The Adventure Continues . . .

Hi! I'm Jackie. I'm an archaeologist. I study ancient treasures to learn about the past.

A few months ago, I found an eight-sided stone in the center of a golden shield. The stone was a magical charm—a talisman!

Legend says that twelve talismans are scattered around the globe. Each one holds a different kind of magic. All twelve talismans together have incredible power!

An evil group called The Dark Hand wants to use the power of the talismans to rule the world! That's why I have to find all the talismans first.

I already have four talismans hidden in a safe place. And I know where there's another one. I saw it on TV!

The problem is, so did The Dark Hand. . . .

A PARACHUTE PRESS BOOK

TM and © 2002 Adelaide Productions, Inc. All Rights Reserved.

Published by Grosset & Dunlap, a division of Penguin Putnam Books for Young Readers, New York. GROSSET & DUNLAP is a trademark of Penguin Putnam, Inc. Published simultaneously in Canada. Printed in U.S.A.

Library of Congress Cataloging-in-Publication Data is available.

ISBN 0-448-42669-2
A B C D E F G H I J

A New Enemy

A novelization by R. S. Ashby
based on the teleplay "Shell Game"
written by Duane Capizzi

Grosset & Dunlap

Chapter 1

"Martial arts lesson Number One," Jackie Chan said to his eleven-year-old niece, Jade. "Learn to breathe deeply."

"I already *know* how to breathe deeply," Jade said. "When do I learn how to chop boards with my bare hands?"

"You need patience for this, Jade," Jackie said. He posed in a fighting stance.

Jade sighed. They had been posing for about an hour. She didn't think she had any patience left! But Jade copied Jackie's position anyway.

"The breath flows to the fingertips," Jackie said calmly. "Then it goes down to the toes."

"And then the toes go up the bad guy's nose!" Jade shouted. "Hee-ya!" She kicked an imaginary bad guy in front of her.

Jackie folded his arms across his chest and stared at her.

"What?" Jade asked innocently. "Wrong pose?"

"You need discipline, Jade," Jackie said sternly.

"But I want to be a lean, mean Jackie Chan machine!" Jade said.

"Don't be in such a hurry," Jackie said. "You know what they say . . . 'slow and steady wins the race.'"

Jade rolled her eyes. "Old Chinese proverb, right?" she asked.

"It's a Greek proverb, actually," Jackie explained. "It's from a story called 'The Tortoise and the Hare.' Once upon a time—" He stopped talking when he saw Jade walking toward the door.

"Where are you going?" Jackie asked.

"Breakfast," Jade called over her shoulder. "See you!"

Jade scurried out of the apartment she lived in with Jackie. Their apartment was special. It was hidden deep within the underground headquarters of Section Thirteen—a top secret group that fought crime.

Jackie was on a special mission for Section Thirteen. His job was to keep twelve ancient Chinese talismans away from an evil group called The Dark Hand. But he had to find them all first!

Each talisman had a magical power. If The Dark Hand got their hands on all twelve, they could control the world!

Jackie had found four talismans so far. They were kept safe in a vault at Section Thirteen. But there were still eight more scattered all over the world.

Jade ran across a high catwalk. On the floor far below, hundreds of

4

secret agents were busy working.

Jade skidded into the kitchen. She saw a box of doughnuts sitting on the table. "Mmm!" She grabbed one and plopped down on a chair.

A television hung on the wall across from her. It was showing the morning news. An enormous tortoise was on the screen.

"His name is Aesop," the news reporter was saying. "He's the latest star at the Bay Aquarium. And this tortoise is special," the reporter went on. "It has something stuck in the middle of its shell."

The camera zoomed in for a closer look. In the tortoise's shell was a round, eight-sided stone with a tiny picture of a pink rabbit on it.

Jade gasped. That's a talisman! she thought. She jumped up from the chair. "Jackieeeeeee!"

Jackie came running into the kitchen. "What? What is it?" he cried.

"I saw a talisman!" Jade said. "It's in the shell of a big tortoise at the Bay Aquarium." She wriggled her hands over her head. "The animal on the talisman had two long ears, like a bunny!"

Jackie thought for a minute. "There *is* a rabbit in the Chinese zodiac," he said. "I will look into it."

"Cool!" Jade said.

"While you're in school," Jackie added.

"Aww!" Jade's shoulders slumped. Jackie never wanted her to help with his missions. He thought she was too young.

I'm going to the aquarium anyway, Jade decided. Jackie will need my help. He just doesn't know it yet!

Someone else was watching TV at the same time as Jade. It was Finn, a member of The Dark Hand.

Finn was sitting on a couch eating a bowl of cereal. He had the TV remote in one hand. He was flipping through all the channels.

A man with ice-blue eyes and a blond ponytail walked up behind Finn. It was Valmont, the leader of The Dark Hand.

Valmont watched as Finn flipped through the channels. Why do I have such lazy people working for me? Valmont wondered. They're not worth the money I pay them.

Valmont watched the television screen as Finn flipped by a game show . . . a commercial for soda . . . a news program about a turtle with an eight-sided stone in its shell . . . a cartoon. . . .

"Stop right there!" Valmont ordered.

"Aahhhh!" Finn jumped up. His milk and cereal spilled everywhere. "Sorry . . . I . . . I didn't see you standing there, sir."

"Go back one channel," Valmont said.

Finn clicked the remote control. The tortoise appeared on the screen again.

Valmont smiled an evil smile. Now he knew where the rabbit talisman was. And somehow he would make sure that he got it.

Chapter 2

That afternoon, Jackie went to the Bay Aquarium to see Aesop, the big tortoise. He walked along the wall of the outdoor aquarium. He passed a penguin exhibit and a cool dolphin tank, too. The tortoise exhibit was just ahead.

Aesop was resting on a sandy island with lots of leafy green trees and bushes.

Two scientists stood talking next

to the tortoise. Jackie crossed a small bridge and headed toward them.

"Hi," he said. He shook hands with the scientists. "I'm Jackie Chan. I'm an archaeologist. I was wondering if I could have a look at the stone in Aesop's shell."

"Sure," one scientist said.

"Thanks." Jackie bent down and examined the eight-sided disk in the center of Aesop's shell. A picture of a pink rabbit was painted on it.

Jackie gasped. "The rabbit talisman," he whispered.

"We haven't figured out what it is yet," one scientist explained. "But we know one thing. It doesn't seem to hurt the tortoise."

"Little girl, this area is off limits,"

the other scientist called out.

Little girl? Jackie thought. He glanced over his shoulder and groaned.

It was Jade. She was standing on the other side of the island. She waved at Jackie.

How did she get here? Jackie wondered. "You're supposed to be at home!" he told Jade. "Doing your *home*work!"

"I *am* doing my homework," Jade insisted. "I'm writing a report on Aesop," she said. "And I'm helping you at the same time," she added with a grin.

Jackie sighed. He walked over to Jade. "You were right," he whispered. "That really *is* a talisman on the tortoise. And if you saw it on TV, we can bet The Dark Hand did, too. They'll probably be here any minute," he said.

Jade rolled her eyes. "Sure. Like bad guys ever watch—"

Boom! The outer wall of the aquarium burst open.

"—TV," Jade finished in a small voice.

Finn rushed through the opening in the wall. Behind him was his partner, Ratso.

Jackie turned to the scientists. "Leave quickly," he said. "And take my niece!"

The scientists led Jade into a nearby building. Jackie tugged at the talisman in Aesop's shell. He had to get the rabbit talisman before The Dark Hand did!

A big shadow fell over Jackie. He looked up.

Standing over Jackie was Tohru, an enforcer for The Dark Hand. He was huge—taller and wider than ten grown men.

"Uh-oh," Jackie said.

Before Jackie could move, Tohru yanked Jackie off the ground, then tossed him over his shoulder.

Jackie landed facedown in the sand. "Okay, time to get tough," he said. He jumped to his feet.

Finn and Ratso rushed at him.

Jackie noticed two buckets of dead fish nearby. He chucked the fish at Finn and Ratso.

"Ewww!" they cried.

Jackie quickly rammed the empty buckets down over their heads, then threw Finn and Ratso into the closest aquarium tank.

Next, Jackie turned to fight Tohru. Tohru simply grabbed Jackie's shirt from behind and threw him into the tank, too!

Jackie opened his eyes underwater. Finn and Ratso were quickly swimming toward him. Jackie struck a fighting pose.

Suddenly, Finn and Ratso stopped short. Then they turned around and started swimming the other way as fast as they could.

Huh? Jackie wondered. Why are Finn and Ratso swimming away?

Jackie glanced behind him.

And then he knew why.

A few feet away was a shark. And it was heading right for Jackie!

Chapter 3

The shark swam faster toward Jackie. It opened its mouth wide, showing rows of sharp teeth.

Jackie froze for a moment, then sprang into action. Thinking fast, he jumped on top of the shark and landed on its back.

The shark twisted and turned. Jackie held on tight as the dangerous creature swam full speed to the water's surface. The shark flung itself

17

into the air and threw Jackie out of the tank!

"Whoa!" Jackie cried as he flew through the air. He landed on the ground with a thud.

"Jackiieee!" Jade yelled. She had come back outside. "You have to save Aesop!"

Jackie saw Tohru pick up the giant tortoise and leave the aquarium through the hole in the wall. Ratso and Finn followed Tohru.

Through the hole, Jackie could see a seaplane floating in the water next to a nearby dock. They were about to get away!

Jackie ran after them, but he wasn't fast enough. Tohru, Finn, and Ratso climbed into the seaplane. A few seconds later, the engine roared, and they took off.

"The rabbit talisman!" Jackie cried. "I've lost it to The Dark Hand!"

Chapter 4

"What do we do now?" Jade asked Jackie a little while later. They were walking down the street away from the aquarium.

"We have to find The Dark Hand enforcers," Jackie answered.

A yellow taxi cab pulled up beside them. "Quick," Jackie told Jade, "jump inside!"

Jade scurried into the taxi.

Instead of getting in behind her,

Jackie slammed the door. The taxi zoomed down the street without him.

"Hey! What's going on?" Jade cried. She turned and saw an old man with tiny, round glasses sitting next to her. It was Uncle.

"Oh, man!" Jade said. She folded her arms accross her chest. Jackie tricked her! He had somehow called Uncle to take her home. This was so unfair!

"So, Jade, how was school?" Uncle asked.

"Just peachy," Jade grumbled. She slumped in her seat.

"One more thing," Uncle went on. "Did Jackie ever find the rabbit talisman? Did he figure out its power?"

Suddenly Jade had an idea. Maybe if she scared Uncle, he'd let her out of the taxi! Jade smiled. She knew just what Uncle was afraid of—evil spirits.

Jade turned to face Uncle. "I am not Jade," she said in a low, deep voice. She raised her hands. "I am an evil spirit. I am Pa-Kung, Ruler of the Rabbit World!"

Uncle stared at her, his eyes wide with fear.

It's working, Jade thought. "I must be set free," she went on. She rolled her eyes back in her head. She waved her hands in the air. "You must release me at once!"

"Stop!" Uncle told the driver. The cab screeched to a halt. Uncle opened the door, and Jade tumbled out onto the sidewalk. The cab quickly drove away.

Jade coughed. "Boy, being a demon is really rough on the throat," she said. "But at least it got me away from Uncle. And now I can help Jackie some more!"

Back at The Dark Hand headquarters, Valmont paced in front of a large statue shaped like a dragon. The statue held the evil spirit of Shendu. Shendu was the real leader of The Dark Hand.

Once Shendu collected all twelve talismans, his spirit would be freed from the statue—free to rule the world!

"You know, Shendu," Valmont said, "finding the talismans is costing me a lot of money. Do you think you could give me some money now? I think it's only fair."

Shendu's eyes glowed red. "Find all twelve talismans for me," the spirit said. "Then you will have more money, gold, and jewels than you can possibly imagine."

Valmont's lips curled. "Where will the money and jewels come from?" he asked. "From the famous lost treasure you keep telling us about? Does that even exist?"

"Ah, so you do not believe in the treasure," Shendu said.

A ninja, clothed in black, silently stepped out of the shadows. He was

24

a member of the Shadowkhan—
Shendu's army of warriors. The ninja
held out a beautiful Chinese cup. It
sparkled with gold and jewels.

Valmont reached eagerly for the
cup. But as soon as he touched it, the
cup melted away.

"Patience, Valmont," the evil spirit
whispered. "Remember—'slow and
steady wins the race!'"

"But, Shendu—" Valmont began.
He was interrupted when Finn, Tohru,
and Ratso burst into the room.

"Hey, Valmont, we scored the rabbit
talisman," Finn boasted. "And we got
the tortoise, too."

"What should we do now?" Tohru
asked.

Valmont stroked his chin. Maybe I

can make some money with the tortoise, he thought.

"Take the tortoise away. Figure out how to remove the talisman from its shell," Valmont ordered his men. "Then prepare to take a little trip to the docks. I know someone who will pay a lot of money for our endangered friend."

A few hours later, Jackie had tracked The Dark Hand thugs to the city docks.

Tohru, Finn, and Ratso were standing on the wooden dock in front of their seaplane. Aesop was on the planks next to them.

Jackie hid behind crates and barrels as he moved closer.

"Looks like we're outnumbered," a girl's voice whispered from behind him.

Jackie gasped and spun around. "Jade!" he cried. Quickly, before anyone could see them, he pulled Jade down behind some crates. "How did you get here? Don't you have a report to write?"

"But I need the tortoise to do it." Jade pointed at Aesop.

"Okay. But stay behind these crates," Jackie whispered. "And keep quiet!"

A moment later, an engine rumbled. Jackie watched as a large ship pulled up to the dock.

A pale man with a black beard got off the boat. He walked down a ramp to the dock. He nodded at Tohru, Finn, and Ratso.

"Are you Carl Nivor?" Finn asked.

The man smiled. "Yes, I am," he said.

Jackie looked closely at Nivor. The man's smile was very creepy.

"Who is this weird guy?" Jade whispered to Jackie.

"Shhh!" Jackie warned her.

Nivor pointed to Aesop. "This must be the tortoise Valmont told me about."

"Yes," Tohru replied. "Now give us the money."

Nivor snapped his fingers. "Boris!"

A short man came down the ramp to the dock. He was holding an open briefcase filled with money. He handed it to the giant Tohru.

"Care to join me for dinner?" Nivor asked The Dark Hand enforcers. "We're having turtle soup."

"Ewww!" Jade said. "He's going to eat soup made from a *turtle?*"

"It's worse than that," Jackie said. "He's going to eat Aesop!"

Chapter 5

"We have to do something to save Aesop!" Jade cried.

"Shhh!" Jackie told Jade. He was trying to hear the men's conversation.

"We can't stay for dinner," Tohru said. "We have to deliver this to Valmont." Tohru held out a small stone disk.

"It's the talisman!" Jackie whispered.

The Dark Hand agents walked down the dock toward the seaplane.

I've got to follow them, Jackie thought. He started to move along the wooden dock.

"Jackie!" Jade cried. She yanked him back behind a barrel. "Where are you going?"

"After the talisman!" Jackie said.

"But what about Aesop?" Jade wailed. "We have to save him from becoming turtle soup!"

"Jade, we don't know what power this talisman has," Jackie explained. "If The Dark Hand gets it, many people could be in danger."

"But we can't get the talisman *and* save Aesop!" Jade said.

"We can do both," Jackie said. "Remember, 'slow and steady wins the race.'"

"Chan?" a man said. "I thought I heard your voice."

Jackie spun around. It was Tohru. Jackie was so busy arguing with Jade that he didn't see The Dark Hand agents sneak right up to them!

In a flash, Jackie tossed Jade up onto a stack of crates where she would be safe.

Ratso jumped in front of Jackie and threw a punch at him.

Jackie leaped aside and flipped Ratso onto the dock.

Ratso threw up his hands in surrender. "Uncle!" he cried.

Confused, Jackie looked around. "Where's Uncle?" he asked.

"Jackie, they're getting away!" Jade cried.

Whirrr! Jackie heard the noise of the seaplane starting to take off. He saw Ratso and Tohru scurry down the dock toward it.

Jackie ran down the dock, too. He leaped through the door of the plane just as Tohru was shutting it.

Before Tohru could react, Jackie grabbed the talisman from him. Then Jackie tried to jump off the plane— but Tohru grabbed his ankle.

"Yaiiiii!" Jackie yelped as he fell and dropped the rabbit talisman.

The talisman flew out the plane's door and onto the dock.

Tohru leaped from the plane and picked it up.

Jackie rushed after Tohru. "Be careful!" he called out. "That talisman

33

will turn you into a chocolate bunny!"

Tohru stopped for a second. He looked at the talisman. Jackie tried to grab it, but Tohru held on tightly.

Suddenly, a ray of light shot out from Tohru's fist!

Uh-oh, Jackie thought. The talisman is working. What's going to happen now?

Chapter 6

Jackie did not have to wait very long to find out. In an instant, Tohru disappeared!

Jackie blinked. Huh? He thought the *snake* talisman turned people invisible.

Flash! Tohru appeared again. Only now, he was way down the dock!

"How'd you get down there so fast?" Jackie called out.

Flash! Tohru disappeared again.

A second later, a big hand tapped

Jackie on the shoulder.

Jackie spun around. It was Tohru! How did he get from there to here so quickly?

As Jackie blocked Tohru's punches, the answer came to him. The rabbit talisman must have the power of super-speed!

Jade climbed down from the crates. She watched as Jackie fought with Tohru on the dock. Even though she wanted to help Jackie, she knew someone who needed her help more. Aesop!

Jade ran down to Nivor's boat and climbed aboard.

Nivor and Boris were both in the galley—the kitchen of the ship.

Aesop was on the floor beside them.

Boris was chopping vegetables and putting them into a bubbling pot on the stove.

Oh, no, Jade thought. That must be the pot they're going to cook Aesop in! She sneaked into a cabinet near the stove, then peeked out to see what was going on.

"Boris, that baked manatee you made last week was delicious," Nivor said. "I can't wait to see what you do with this tortoise." He smacked his lips. "I'll be in the study until dinner."

"Okay, boss," Boris said as Nivor walked out of the galley.

Boris studied a recipe book on the counter. "All I need now is a pinch of salt, a dash of pepper—and one big tortoise," he said.

He turned and headed to a pantry off the kitchen.

Now is my chance to save Aesop, Jade thought. She quietly climbed out of the cabinet and tiptoed up behind the tortoise.

"Come on, Aesop," she whispered. "We've got to get out of here right away! You're the next ingredient!" She pushed the tortoise with all her might.

Aesop didn't budge.

Then Jade heard footsteps. Boris was coming back from the pantry!

"At least I can stop the soup from cooking," Jade said. She turned the knob on the stove. The flames under the pot went out. Then she dove back into the cabinet.

When Boris returned, he stared at the pot on the stove. "That's strange," he said. "The water should be boiling by now. How did the burner go out?"

Boris turned the knob on the stove and started the fire again. He began chopping carrots, then suddenly stopped.

"Oops! I forgot the most important thing." He rushed back to the pantry.

As soon as he was gone, Jade climbed out of the cabinet again. Got to hurry, she thought. This is my last chance to get Aesop out of here!

She tried pushing the tortoise again. "Come on, Aesop!" she cried. But Aesop still didn't move.

Jade heard Boris coming back. She jumped behind a counter and peeked out.

. Then she gasped.

Boris was walking toward her, holding a huge, sharp knife!

Chapter 7

Boris bent over the tortoise—and raised the knife high in the air.

No way am I going to let him chop up Aesop! Jade thought. She jumped out from behind the counter. "Stop!" she yelled.

At first, Boris seemed surprised. Then he glared at Jade.

"Um . . . pretty please?" Jade asked, trying to smile.

Boris didn't smile back. Instead,

he grabbed Jade and pulled her into the study.

Nivor glanced up from his newspaper when they came in. "Who is this?" he asked Boris.

"Let Aesop go, you tortoise-eating creep!" Jade demanded.

Nivor raised one eyebrow. "Such a delightful child!" he said. "She'd go well with a nice cream sauce."

"What?" Jade yelled. "Let me out of here!"

Nivor gave her a nasty grin. "Only joking." He turned to Boris. "Now lock her up, and finish cooking my dinner!"

While Jade was locked up, Jackie was still fighting with Tohru on the dock.

"Who's a chocolate bunny now?" Tohru asked Jackie. He tried to punch Jackie with one huge hand.

Jackie jumped aside. He lifted a leg to kick Tohru.

Flash! Tohru disappeared. Then he reappeared behind Jackie and knocked him down with a fist.

Flash! Tohru disappeared again.

A second later, Jackie spotted him halfway down the dock. He was getting away!

How can I stop him if I can't see him? Jackie wondered. Then he spotted a barrel of oil nearby and got an idea.

Jackie jumped to his feet. He yanked the lid off the barrel of oil and kicked it over. Oil spilled across the dock.

43

"Whaaa!" Tohru yelled. He slipped on the oil and slid across the dock—until he slammed into the side of the seaplane. The talisman slipped out of Tohru's hand and landed on the dock.

Tohru and the seaplane sank into the water!

Jackie ran to get the talisman. He picked it up and held it tightly.

Now it's time to save Aesop, he thought. "Jade?" he called out. He looked all around the dock. But Jade was nowhere to be found.

Vroom! Jackie heard the motor of Carl Nivor's boat. It was moving quickly away from the dock.

Then Jackie had a horrible thought. What if Jade tried to save Aesop all by herself? What if she was on Nivor's ship?

Jackie had to find out. He dove into the water and squeezed the rabbit talisman with all his might. The talisman beamed out bright rays of light.

And Jackie glided across the water faster than a torpedo!

He slammed right into the side of the boat. "Ouch!" he cried.

Jade's face appeared in a tiny round window nearby. "Jackie! I'm in here!" she called out.

A moment later, Jackie boarded the ship and found Jade.

"Wow!" Jade said. "How'd you get all the way out here so fast?"

Jackie held up the rabbit talisman.

"With this," he said. "*Now* we can rescue the tortoise." He shook a finger at Jade. "It's as I said: 'Slow and steady wins the race.'"

Back at The Dark Hand headquarters, Valmont and Tohru faced an angry Shendu. Tohru was drying himself off with a towel.

"Valmont, you and your men are supposed to find talismans, not sell pets!" the statue snarled.

"Perhaps if you gave me some money up front," Valmont said, "I wouldn't have to sell pets."

Shendu's eyes glowed an evil red. *Whoosh!* Flames shot from the statue's mouth.

Valmont and Tohru leaped out of

the fire's path just in time.

Tohru gasped. "I didn't know he could do that."

Valmont kneeled on the floor in front of the statue. "I promise, Shendu," he said, "we will get the rabbit talisman back from Chan. It will be yours."

Shendu's eyes flashed red. "I will make sure of it," he said. An army of ninja warriors fluttered out of the shadows. An army of Shadowkhan!

Chapter 8

Jackie and Jade tiptoed into the doorway of the ship's galley. Boris was at the counter. He gave his knife one last polish, then raised it high above the tortoise.

"Aesop!" Jade cried.

Jackie squeezed the talisman. *Flash!* He zoomed in front of Boris and grabbed the knife.

"The kitchen is now closed," Jackie said. "No turtle soup today!"

Thunk! Jackie threw the knife into the wall.

"Who are you?" Boris asked.

Jackie didn't answer. He used his super-speed to pick up Boris and lock him in the pantry. Then he quickly turned to help Jade.

"Let's get going, Aesop!" Jade said. "Move!"

Jackie and Jade pushed with all their strength. But the huge tortoise didn't budge.

Suddenly, Jackie heard a strange fluttering sound all around him. He gulped, knowing exactly what that sound meant. The Shadowkhan were on the boat!

Seconds later, ten ninja warriors circled around Jade and Jackie.

"It's time for super-rabbit super-speed," Jackie told Jade. He closed his hand around the talisman.

Flash! Jackie landed in front of a ninja and pounded him with a flying kick.

Wham! Wham! Wham! Jackie ran through the galley, knocking down three more Shadowkhan.

Zing! A Shadowkhan threw a ninja star at Jackie. With his super-speed, Jackie grabbed a frying pan to block the sharp, dangerous weapon.

Jade watched the battle from behind the counter. She knew she had to get Aesop out of the kitchen while Jackie was fighting. But how?

Jade's gaze darted around the kitchen, then landed on some carrots lying on the counter. That's it! she thought. I'll get Aesop to move by holding carrots in front of his face. Tortoises love carrots, right?

Jade grabbed a bunch of carrots and held them over Aesop's beak. She took a step backward.

Aesop stared at the carrots. He took a step forward.

"Yes!" Jade cheered. "It's working!"

Jade walked backward through the kitchen, still dangling the carrots. Aesop followed her out the door.

"Come on, Aesop," Jade said softly. "Keep going—oops!"

Jade didn't realize that she had walked backward all the way to the door of the study. When she looked up, she saw Carl Nivor staring right at her!

Jade gulped. She held out the carrots to Nivor. "Want one?" she asked.

Nivor stood up from his chair. "I want my dinner!" he growled.

"Jackiieee!" Jade cried. She ran back into the galley. There, she saw a Shadowkhan warrior about to fire an arrow at Jackie!

Jackie jumped aside, and the arrow struck a big can of olive oil. The oil squirted all over the kitchen.

"Whoa!" Jackie slipped. The talisman flew out of his hand, and landed next to Jade's foot.

I have to help Jackie and Aesop get out of here! Jade thought. And she needed the super-speed power of the rabbit talisman to do it!

Jade grabbed the talisman. Then

she ran down the hall to Aesop. She snapped the rabbit talisman back into Aesop's shell and hopped onto his back.

"Let's go!" she cried.

Jade and Aesop soared down the hall.

"Super-Tortoise to the rescue!" she shouted. Faster than a speeding rabbit, Jade and Aesop zoomed into the galley. They grabbed Jackie and swooped him up.

"Good timing," Jackie said. He held on to the back of the tortoise as they zoomed off the ship and onto the dock.

"I figured you might need my help," Jade said. She grinned. "And you were right. We were able to rescue the rabbit talisman *and* save Aesop!"

"As I always say," Jackie said. "'slow and steady wins the race!'"

A letter to you from Jackie

Dear Friends,

In <u>A New Enemy</u>, Jade thinks that we can't possibly save Aesop the tortoise and also rescue the rabbit talisman. But I tell her an old Greek proverb I learned a long time ago: "slow and steady wins the race."

I believe in this motto just as much today as I did when I was a child. When I was a young student all I wanted was to be a famous actor. But my dream did not come true for many years. As a result, I learned the value of patience.

While I was in school, I acted in many small movies—so many, I can't even remember the names of some of them! But I stayed patient. I told myself that making these movies was great practice. I was convinced that slowly but surely I'd get to make bigger ones. And when I <u>did</u> have that opportunity, I knew I'd be prepared.

When I was offered my first big role, I used the skills that I'd learned to make my performance the best it could be. All of my practice finally paid off, and the movie was a great success.

Now, whenever I star in a movie, I make sure

that all my stunts are done with safety and with patience. It's not always easy. In one movie, it took me hundreds of tries to get a stunt right. That was the greatest number of takes in any movie I'd ever done! Even though people wanted me to give up, I knew that I could do it, and I finally did.

So, the next time you think you can't accomplish something, remember the old Greek proverb. If you take your time and believe in yourself, you can do anything!

JACKIE CHAN

Find out what happens in the next book

#7 Revenge of The Dark Hand

Valmont, the leader of The Dark Hand, has the power of the dragon talisman. The power to destroy anything in his way—including Jackie!

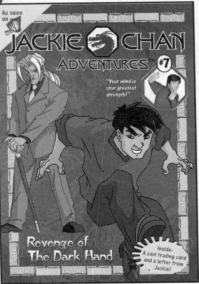

JACKIE CHAN
ADVENTURES™